Don't Be Picky, Clover!

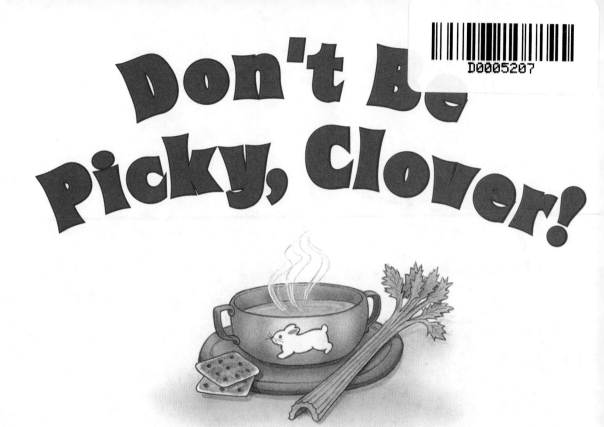

by **Rita Balducci**

illustrated by **Cathy Beylon**

inchworm
PRESS
TM

Clover was the youngest of Mama Bunny's ten little children, and the pickiest, too. While all the other bunnies were in and out of the library in a hop, Clover spent hours selecting just the right book.

LIBRARY
HOURS
MON.-FRI
10:00-6:00
SAT.-SUN.
10:00-4:00

Her sisters and brothers were always finished with their drawings while Clover was still picking her first crayon.

"That's our Clover," Mama Bunny always said with a sigh.

When it came to eating, Clover was pickier than ever. She had grown choosier and choosier until the only food that had the right smell, the right color, and the right taste was celery soup. Clover ate celery soup for breakfast, lunch, and dinner — and sometimes even for an afternoon snack.

Mama Bunny tried not to worry. She hoped Clover would get tired of celery soup and start eating carrots and beans and cabbage like a good little bunny.

"Clover, dear, won't you try some turnip?" Mama asked sweetly.

"YUCK!" Clover said with a sniff.

Clover's brothers and sisters ate all their vegetables. "Yummm!" they said, licking their lips. "This carrot is deee-licious!"

But they weren't fooling Clover. There was no way she was going to eat a carrot!

Finally, Mama Bunny decided to ask Grandma Bunny for some help.

Grandma Bunny smiled when she heard Mama's story. "Clover sounds like another little bunny I knew a long time ago," she chuckled. "You send her over to me. I think I know just the thing to do."

And so, the very next morning, Mama Bunny sent Clover over to visit Grandma.

"Good morning!" Grandma cried, wrapping Clover in a big bunny-hug. "You're just in time to help me in my garden." Grandma handed Clover a little basket. "Let's see what looks good for dinner."

"That's easy," Clover said. "Celery!"

Grandma nodded. "Oh, sure," she replied. "But there's more to eating than that."

Clover shook her head. "Not for me, there isn't. I only eat celery soup!"

"Is that so?" Grandma asked with a grin. "Well, then we'll make celery soup for you."

Grandma's garden was blooming with brightly colored vegetables — red beets, orange carrots, green cucumbers, and yellow corn. But Clover only had eyes for the tall, pale stalks of celery.

"I'll pick the celery!" she declared. When Clover had picked plenty of celery, she noticed Grandma was filling her basket with many different kinds of vegetables. "What are you doing, Grandma? We don't need beans and onions and lettuce for celery soup."

"Well, Clover, we're only making celery soup for you. I'm having Surprise Soup. It's full of all different kinds of vegetables. The taste they make together is always a delicious surprise. Would you like to help me pick these tomatoes?"

Clover thought for a moment. There didn't seem to be any harm in picking different vegetables as long as she didn't have to eat them. So Clover and Grandma spent a happy hour picking tomatoes, onions, and many other vegetables for Surprise Soup.

Back in the house, Clover and Grandma began to rinse the vegetables they had gathered. Then Grandma put two pots of water on the stove. To one pot, Grandma added the celery that Clover had picked. "Your celery soup will be done soon," she said.

"Would you like to know a secret, Clover?" Grandma asked.

"A secret?" Clover exclaimed, her eyes widening. Clover loved secrets.

"Yes, lots of bunnies have asked me for my recipe for Surprise Soup, but I've always kept it a secret. With all the help you've given me in picking the ingredients, I think you deserve to know my secret recipe."

Clover felt very special. "What do you do first?" she asked eagerly.

So Grandma showed Clover how to carefully break apart the different vegetables and add them to the pot. Then she showed Clover the special spices she used. Clover added the spices and stirred.

"Time for a taste!" Grandma said, dipping her ladle in.

Clover knew it wasn't celery soup, but it was starting to smell good. Still, she had been a picky eater for so long she was afraid to try something new. She said, "No thank you. I only eat celery soup."

Grandma grinned. "You know, Clover," she whispered, "when your Mama was just a little bunny, she never liked to eat anything but turnip pudding!"

Clover looked up in surprise. "But she eats all sorts of things now!" she cried.

"Oh, sure," Grandma said. "She figured out that she'd rather try new things than just sit around wondering what she was missing. She's a smart one, your Mama."

Clover squirmed. Didn't Grandma think that she was a smart one, too?

At last it was dinnertime. Grandma set two pretty bowls on the table while Clover got the glasses and silverware. Grandma ladled out some Surprise Soup for herself, and some celery soup for Clover.

"I've been looking forward to this all day!" Grandma said.

Clover tasted her celery soup. It tasted the same as it always did, but somehow not as delicious as she remembered. She looked at Grandma enjoying the Surprise Soup—the soup that Clover had gathered the vegetables for, stirred in the pot, added spices to, and learned a whole secret recipe for!

"Grandma," Clover announced, "I would like some Surprise Soup." Without a word, Grandma poured Clover a new bowl of Surprise Soup.

Clover closed her eyes, wrinkled her nose, and took the tiniest, teensiest taste of the soup. Then her eyes flew open. "It's good!" she said, sinking her spoon in for more.

The next day, Clover surprised Mama Bunny by offering to make dinner for the family. "I have the secret recipe for Surprise Soup!" Clover exclaimed.

Mama smiled at her littlest bunny. "I can't wait to try it!" she told her.

And so Clover spent the rest of the day cooking and preparing while the rest of the family enjoyed the delicious smells from the kitchen.

"Dinnertime!" Clover cried.

Clover held her breath as Mama and the rest of the bunnies tasted the soup.

"It's delicious!" the bunnies shouted. "But . . . it tastes different from Grandma's!"

"That's because this is my secret recipe," Clover explained. "My secret ingredients are . . ."

"Turnips!" Mama cried.

"And carrots, and beans, and cabbage, and tomatoes," Clover laughed. "But guess what I didn't put in?"

"Celery!" shouted her brothers and sisters.

Clover nodded, folding her arms. "I chose my own ingredients!" she declared.

"That's our Clover," Mama Bunny said with a smile.

The Ghost Who Was Afraid of the Dark

by **Alex Okin**

illustrated by **Carolyn Bracken**

inchworm
PRESS ™

New York

In a big old house on top of a hill there lived a young ghost named Spookie. Spookie and his parents lived in the attic. A human family lived in the rest of the house. Spookie was allowed out of the attic only in the daytime because he was too young to spook at night.

During the day Spookie liked to float from one bright, sunny room to another. His favorite places to visit were the children's rooms. He would play with their dolls and trucks and stuffed animals while they were at school. Sometimes he forgot to put the toys away — but usually he remembered.

One afternoon when Spookie returned to the attic, his mother said, "It's time you learned how to haunt at night, dear."

"Really?" said Spookie, feeling a bit nervous. "But don't you think the night is too dark for a little ghost like me?"

"You've grown quite a bit this past year," said his father. "It's time you act like a big ghost and learn how to scare the humans at night."

"And remember, dear, at night we get to wear our chains and rattle them around when we haunt," said his mother.

"But I'm not used to the dark," said Spookie. "I've never even stayed up past sunset."

"Big ghosts don't sleep at night, dear," his mother said. "You'll get used to the dark."

That night when the coast was clear, Spookie followed his parents through the attic door. The house was dark and still, and the humans were asleep in their beds.

"Follow us," said Spookie's father. "We'll show you the best places to hide and haunt."

They drifted into the musty old library. "I'm scared," Spookie whispered. "It's too dark in here."

"Shhh," said his mother. "You'll be okay."

But Spookie couldn't keep quiet. Before he knew it, he was crying, "Boo-hoo! Boo-hoo!" Suddenly the ghosts heard a door open upstairs. Then they heard the humans moving around.

"Quick, Spookie, hide behind these curtains," said his mother.
Spookie's parents began to blow with all their might. The
howling of their voices masked the sound of Spookie's cries.
The curtains flapped loudly in the breeze.

"Not to worry. It's just the wind," said a voice upstairs.
Soon the humans were quiet again.

When they were back in the light of the hallway, Spookie's
father whispered, "Now Spookie, I want you to float into the
little girl's bedroom and hide in her toy closet."

"But what if I knock something over? What if I start to cry and I wake everyone up?" Spookie asked.

"You'll be fine. The dark is not going to hurt you," said his mother.

Spookie dashed through the door of the little girl's bedroom, and let out a sigh of relief when he saw that she slept with a tiny night-light on.

The toy closet was the darkest place he had ever been in by himself. Spookie shook so much with fear that his chains began to rattle. He tried hard not to cry, but he just couldn't help himself. Finally he whimpered, "Boo-hoo! Boo-hoo!"

The little girl woke up and started to cry, too. The sound surprised Spookie because when the little girl cried, she sounded just like him!

The little girl's parents rushed into her room. "Why are you crying, dear?" they asked her.

"There's a ghost in my room!" cried the little girl.

"There, there. You must have been dreaming," said her parents as they tucked her back into bed.

"I want my dolly," the little girl said. "I can't go back to sleep without my dolly."

"Where *is* your dolly?" her mother asked.

The little girl looked sad. "I don't know," she said. "She's lost."

The mother went into the toy closet to look for the doll.
Spookie quietly floated up and out of the closet, over her
head. She didn't even see him.

When the little girl's mother couldn't find the doll anywhere, she picked up a stuffed bear. "How about sleeping with Fuzzy instead?"

The little girl shook her head. "I want my dolly."

Suddenly Spookie remembered that he had been playing with the doll earlier that day. He must have forgotten to put it back where it belonged.

"I'll get it!" he whispered to himself.

Spookie floated under the little girl's bed where the doll
was lying. Luckily the little girl's parents were so busy
comforting her that they didn't notice him.

Spookie carefully pushed the doll out from under the
bed until it was laying beside the mother's foot.

"Oh, here she is," exclaimed the mother a moment later.

"Thank you, Mommy!" cried the little girl, hugging the
doll. "I'm so happy you found her."

Me, too, thought Spookie. Hearing the little girl's happy
voice made Spookie forget to be afraid of the darkness
under the bed.

Back in the attic, Spookie told his parents that when he was under the little girl's bed he wasn't afraid of the dark at all.

"We're very proud of you, dear," said his mother. "Now that you're not afraid of the dark anymore you can haunt with us every night."

Spookie snuggled against his soft quilt, and felt very grown-up. He didn't want to spook at night. He wanted to help people instead. "That will be my special secret," he whispered out loud. Then he drifted off to sleep.